D1010289

For my mother,
Dorothy

BLUE APPLE BOOKS

Copyright © 2011 Daniel Cleary
Balloon Toons® is a registered
trademark of Harriet Ziefert, Inc.
All rights reserved/CIP data is available.
Published in the United States 2011 by
Blue Apple Books
515 Valley Street, Maplewood, NJ 07040
www.blueapplebooks.com

First Edition
Printed in China
HC ISBN: 978-1-60905-080-1
2 4 6 8 10 9 7 5 3 1
PB ISBN: 978-1-60905-185-3
2 4 6 8 10 9 7 5 3 1

I'm Prickles.
I'm Squeeky.
I'm nobody.

Squeeky, who is that next to the fish bowl?
Umm... a fish burglar?

There is no such thing as a fish burglar.
Are you sure?
You're hiding dust bunnies again, aren't you?
I told you to take them outside.
I tried. They won't go.

Don't look under the couch!
All right, who's under there?
Nobody.

Prickles, don't make them come out. They're afraid!
Out!

Why not? What are they afraid of?
They've never seen the light of day.

We did try looking out the window. But then we got scared and ran back under the couch.

You know the rules. No dust bunnies are allowed on my floors.

Hey, wait a minute. How many of you are under there?
We're not sure. A bunch of us are stuck in a clump.

Then unclump yourselves, and march over to that door!
No! Not the outside!
Please, don't make us!

It's too bright out there!
Squeeky, help us, please!

Prickles! They're afraid!
Don't you Prickles me!

What's to be afraid of?
It's a beautiful day.
There's nothing out there but a yard full of green grass.
Grass scares us.

Oh, for goodness sakes. It's grass. It doesn't bite.
But grass is so shiny.
And so green, it hurts our eyes.

And there's no place to hide.
You're all very clever. I'm sure you'll have no trouble finding places to hide.
Can't we at least wait until dark?
No! You have to go now. I know your tricks.

Come on, Squeeky. Take their little dusty hands.

The Big Cheese will be home any minute. This house must be squeaky clean when he arrives.

Please, Prickles! Let us stay. We won't make any noise!
It's not the noise that bothers me.
It's your dirty, clumpy, fuzzy habit of lying about that I can't put up with.

How about if we stand in a straight line against the wall, like this?
Look, we're not even touching.
And no clumps!
No more excuses. Out!

How about wallpaper? We make a great wallpaper.

The Big Cheese will never even know we're here.
But, I'll know you're here.
Hey, look what else we can do!

Watch us squeeze ourselves together into one tiny, itsy-bitsy ball.
I'll call the circus. I hear they're looking for new acts.
Awesome!

Look, we're practically invisible!
No you're not! You're still a furry ball of dust in the middle of my spotless living room floor.
Now march!

Squeeky, help us!
Prickles, I can't make them leave. They're my best friends!
Who else but you would make friends with balls of dust?
Lots of people!
You make it sound like dirt is bad.

So what if we're a little fuzzy looking and have a few funny spots and speckles. Nobody's perfect.
We're real.
We're interesting.
We're organic.
We're made from all kinds of neat stuff.

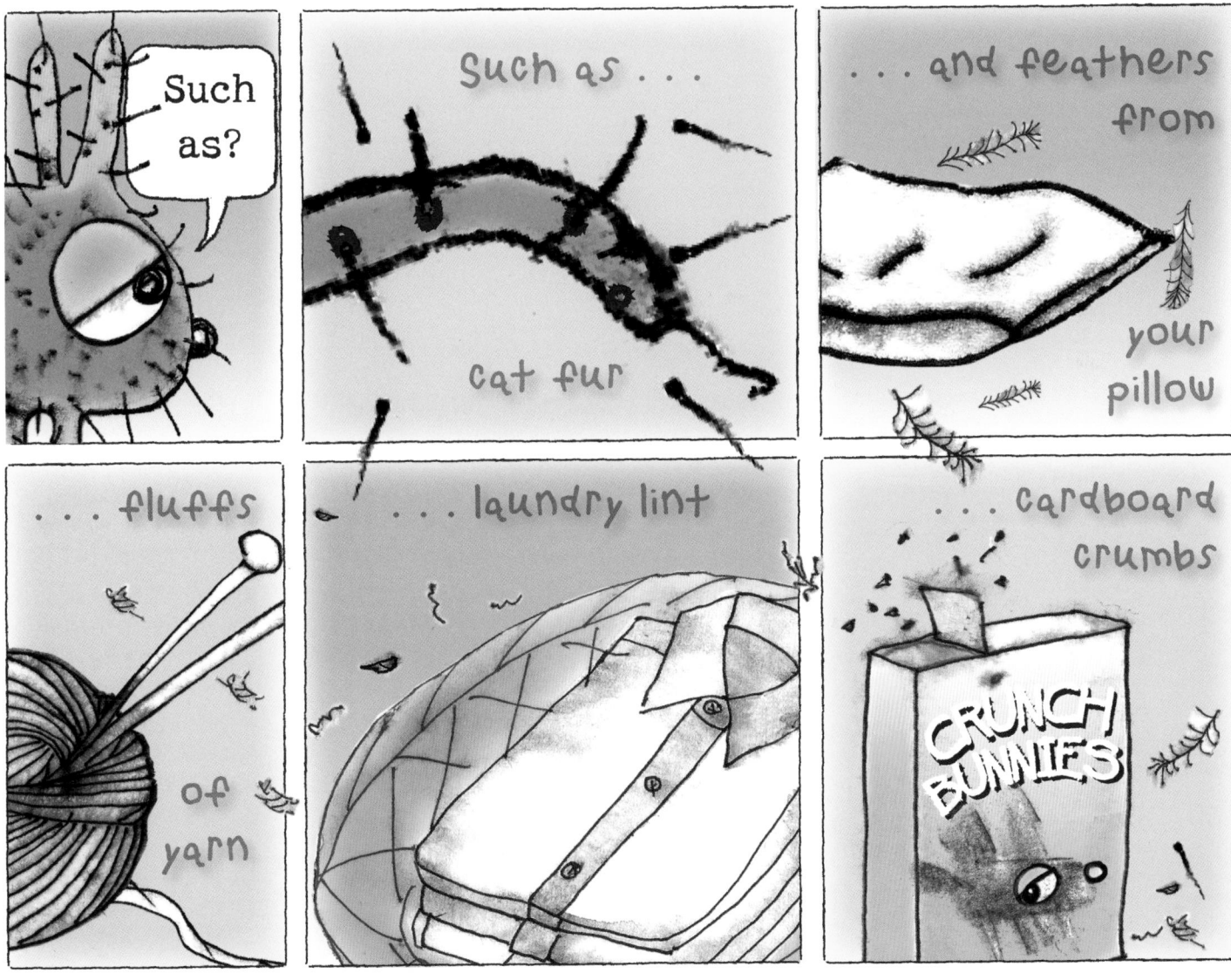
Such as?
Such as . . .
cat fur
. . . and feathers from
your pillow
. . . fluffs
of yarn
. . . laundry lint
. . . cardboard crumbs
CRUNCH BUNNIES

And all held together with our good friend Spidy's old cobwebs!
We're all natural.
If you're so natural, you should have no problem playing outside in the dirt.
Hi!

But we don't know anything about outside dirt. We're house bunnies!
There's the Big Cheese now. I don't have time for this nonsense!

I'm getting the vacuum.
Not the vacuum!
Squeeky, hurry! You have to do something!
Okay!
There is one last thing . . .
Quick! Follow me!

Welcome home, Mr. Cheese.
How was your trip?
Grumble. Grumble. Growl. Growl.

Hello, my little fishies.
Hmmm . . . Interesting sweater, Squeeky.
Thanks.

Now, Prickles, about that turtleneck you knitted for Squeeky . . .
Oh, but no! Mr. Cheese, I didn't . . .
I'd love one in my size.
But . . .

It will take me forever. He's gigantic!
Don't worry, Prickles. There are plenty more dust bunnies.
Come on out, guys!

Awesome! Let's start knitting.
I told you they were awesome.